The Nature Club
We All Are One

Text copyright © 2019 by Rachel Mazur
Cover illustrations copyright © 2019 by Elettra Cudignotto
Inside illustrations copyright © 2019 by Rachelle Dyer
Edited by Emma Irving and Julie Mazur Tribe

A portion of the proceeds from the sale of this book will
benefit environmental education.

Library of Congress Cataloging-in-Publication Data is
available upon request.
ISBN 978-1-7329156-4-0 (paperback)
ISBN 978-1-7329156-9-5 (ebook)

First edition 2019

10 9 8 7 6 5 4 3 2 1

WILD BEAR
P R E S S

Wild Bear Press operates on the simple premise
that nature-based stories connect children with
the natural world and inspire them to protect it.

Visit us on the Web! www.natureclubbooks.com

The Nature Club
We All Are One

Rachel Mazur

WILD BEAR PRESS

For Marlo, because we are always
connected—even when
we are far apart

1

"Next stop, Greenley Station. *Fiiiiiive* minutes," the conductor announced as he hurried through the train. "Please gather near the doors. It will be a short stop."

"That's our stop," Miguel said to his mother, who was eyeing him questioningly.

"*Estamos allá,*" she translated while poking her husband in the row ahead of them. Miguel's dad was the only one in the family who didn't speak any English, except a few words for greetings and directions. He nodded and stood up quickly to lower their bags from the overhead racks.

"*Haber le ayudo Papá,*" Miguel said, jumping up to help his father. Together, they lowered their three suitcases while Miguel's mother gathered the waste from their café car lunch of pizza, soft pretzels, and soda.

"So much waste," she said, shaking her head.

1

"Where should I put it?"

"There's a garbage can down near the bathroom. I'll take it," Miguel said, grabbing the pile of trash from her and then making his way down the aisle. He threw the non-recyclable trash into the garbage but tossed the empty bottles into the blue bin next to it. "At least part of our lunch isn't going into a landfill," he said to himself.

Miguel then rejoined his parents to grab his soccer ball and suitcase and help them stumble down the aisle with their luggage while the train rattled along.

"Now arriving at Greenley Station," the conductor's voice crackled over the speaker. The train's bells rang loudly until, finally, the train screeched into the station. As it lurched to a halt, Miguel's mother fell against him.

"*Mamá*! Are you okay?" he asked.

"Oh yes, except . . . ," she stopped, realizing she had knocked her glasses off. Quickly shoving them back onto her head, she put them on upside down, sending Miguel into a fit of laughter.

"What, you don't like them like this?" asked his mother, joining him in laughter until they both had tears in their eyes. Although Señor Ramirez looked at them crossly, Miguel was grateful for the laugh. It gave him some relief from the edginess he'd felt all day. It had been many hours of travel by plane and then train to get from his home in Nicaragua to Izzy's town in Northern California.

His parents had been invited to attend a meeting of organic coffee growers in San Francisco. As a leader in converting conventional coffee farms to organic, his mother was even asked to give the closing speech at the Friday night banquet.

Although Señor and Señora Ramirez had five children, Miguel was their youngest and the only one who still lived with them. Since Miguel had a pen pal, Izzy Philips, who lived in California, his parents had decided to bring him on the trip so he could visit her in person.

Izzy's mom, Mrs. Philips, had offered to pick

Miguel up in San Francisco, but Señora Ramirez insisted on delivering him herself. After all, it was Miguel's first time outside of Nicaragua *and* his first time away from his parents for a whole week.

As Miguel stepped off the train, his stomach felt tight and queasy. He took a deep breath, telling himself it was just nerves, and then helped his parents down from the train and onto the platform.

"*Espero que ellos no te olviden,*" his father worried, looking around.

"*No se preocupe Papá,*" said Miguel. "Izzy will not forget me." Just as he said that, a girl with straight, brown hair pulled back into a ponytail pulling a younger boy with bright-red hair by the hand ran up to them, asking, "Are you Miguel?"

"Izzy!" Miguel responded, smiling broadly.

"I'm so glad you're here," Izzy said and gave him an awkward hug.

"Me too!" he responded. Miguel then put his arm warmly around the boy, saying, "And you must be Zack."

"How did you know?" Zack asked.

"By your penguin," Miguel said, nodding toward the large stuffed penguin Zack was holding tightly in his right arm. "Izzy says Otto is always with you."

"Oh," Zack said, smiling.

"And by your *enyesado*," Miguel said, nodding toward the orange cast on Zack's left arm.

"You have a great memory," Izzy said with a laugh. She then straightened and looked at Miguel's parents. "Hi. I mean, um, *bienvenidos Señor y Señora Ramírez*," she mumbled self-consciously.

Before they could answer, Mrs. Philips walked up carrying Izzy's littlest brother, Carson, in her arms. "Welcome!" she said to Señor and Señora Ramirez. "We are so happy to finally meet you. Izzy so values her friendship with Miguel and is thrilled to spend a week with him."

"Thank you. Miguel feels the same about Izzy, and I am so happy to meet you, too," Señora Ramirez said while her husband watched awkwardly. Miguel and Izzy's teachers had set them up as pen pals over two years earlier, so Izzy could practice writing in Spanish and Miguel could practice writing in English while they learned about each other's cultures. While most kids in their classes had stopped writing to their pen pals long ago, Miguel and Izzy had kept writing and had formed a strong friendship.

Turning to Señor Ramirez, Mrs. Philips asked, "How is your . . . um, I mean, well, do you speak any English?"

"*Un poco*," he answered. "*Muy poco*."

"And I don't speak a word of Spanish," Mrs. Philips said apologetically.

"Don't worry about him," Miguel's mom said. "I'll translate for him. Or we can just ignore him." She laughed while Señor Ramirez rolled his eyes, knowing her well enough to assume the joke was on him.

"I'll let that be *your* call," Mrs. Philips said, smiling. "Now, for planning purposes, what time is your train back to San Francisco?"

"It leaves at seven o'clock," Miguel's mom replied. "We already have tickets."

"Oh no, that only gives us an hour. I was hoping to make you a nice meal at our house, but given the limited time, let's just grab something to eat at the station café.

"That sounds fine," Miguel's mom said. "Although we only need something to drink," she added, patting her stomach. "We ate the entire way here."

The two families wandered over to the café and enjoyed a drink together. While the others had lemonade served in frosted glass mugs, Miguel ordered a bottle of cold soda. He hoped the bubbles would settle his gurgling stomach.

Then it was time for Señor and Señora Ramirez to head back to the city. The Philipses wished them a good trip and they exchanged contact information. They waited at the café while Miguel tossed his bottle into the recycling bin before helping his parents onto their train.

"*Sé bueno y escucha a la Señora Philips*," Señor

Ramirez said, handing Miguel some money for the week and giving him a big hug.

"*Por supuesto, Papa, no se preocupe. Lo amo,*" Miguel replied. Then he turned to his mother. "Good luck, *Mamá*. I know you will be a great speaker."

"I hope you are right. If only the California governor would come! Then I could make a real *diferencia*," she said.

"If he is smart, he will come, learn, and make things better," Miguel said.

Señora Ramirez smiled at her son and hugged him tightly. "*Te amo Mijo*, I will miss you. Have a great time and please, call us every night! We will see you next Sunday."

"Don't worry, *Mamá*. I will. *Te amo Mamá*."

The conductor announced that all visitors needed to exit the train. Miguel gave his parents one last hug and then stepped back down onto the platform, where he waved until the train was out of sight.

2

Miguel took a deep breath and headed back to the café, where the Philipses were waiting.

"Let's head back to our house and get you settled in," Mrs. Philips suggested as she lifted his suitcase into the trunk.

"Thank you, Mrs. Philips," Miguel said.

As they drove through town, Izzy pointed out the Greenley elementary and middle schools, the Greenley Grocery, and their favorite place to get sandwiches, Green Deli.

"Does everything here have the word 'green' in its name?"

"Not the Clementine Inn," Zack said, pointing to a hotel as they drove past.

"But the other hotel in town is named the Green Dragon Inn," Mrs. Philips said with a laugh.

"Speaking of green, can we stop at Green

County Park to show Miguel?" Izzy asked.

"Tonight?" Mrs. Philips asked.

"Yes!" Zack said. "He has to see the park."

"Can't it wait until tomorrow?" Mrs. Philips asked. "It's almost dark."

"Miguel won't have truly arrived until he sets foot in the park. It's the Nature Club's home base," Izzy said.

Izzy, Zack, and their friends Brooke and Tai had formed the Nature Club at the beginning of the summer, with Miguel an honorary member. Their idea was to learn all about nature—mostly wildlife—and then work to protect it. Green County Park was ground zero for the club.

"Well, why not?" Mrs. Philips responded, and within minutes pulled into a gravel parking lot.

"Already?" Miguel asked.

"Oh yeah," Izzy laughed. "Greenley is a *really* small town."

"Our house is right down the street," Mrs. Philips added, "but this is where Izzy and Zack will have you spending the week. I'm glad we stopped. It's beautiful here in the evening."

They got out of the car and looked around. The sun had just set and the trees appeared as black silhouettes against the darkening sky. It was also quiet. All they could hear were crickets, a light wind, and the occasional shuffling of their feet on the gravel. Then a car approached from the distance.

As it passed, the headlights lit up the yellowish eyes of an animal at the edge of the meadow. The animal hesitated for just a moment and then moved into the bushes.

"Did you see that?" Zack asked the others.

"I did," Miguel said. "It looked like a wild cat."

"That's exactly what it was," Izzy said. "A bobcat."

"Awesome!" Zack said. "I've never seen a bobcat before."

"Me neither," Mrs. Philips added.

"Miguel, you must be good luck!" Izzy said.

"I think he is," Mrs. Philips agreed. "You kids are in for a great week. Miguel, how did you know it was a wild cat?"

"It was too big to be a house cat, so I knew it was a wild cat," Miguel said. "But I wouldn't have known it was a bobcat. The wild cats in Nicaragua are different than the ones here. Izzy, how did you know it was a bobcat?"

"Here we only have two types of wild cats: mountain lions, which are big and have really long tails, and bobcats, which are small and have short tails like this one had. That's how I knew," Izzy said.

"Don't we also have ring-tailed cats?" Mrs. Philips asked.

"We do, but they are small and have long striped tails. And they aren't even cats—they are in the raccoon family," Izzy explained.

"No kidding," Mrs. Philips said.

"I want to see a ringtail cat," Zack said.

"How about if we start by feeling lucky about seeing a bobcat?" Mrs. Philips said. "In all my years, I've never seen one before. I'd heard they were around, but didn't really believe it."

"Did you see how its eyes lit up?" Zack asked.

"Their eyes don't light up—they reflect light," Izzy said.

"How?" Zack asked.

"You know that bobcats are nocturnal, right?" Izzy asked.

"Yup," Zack answered.

"Well, nocturnal animals' eyes reflect light. It's called eyeshine," she said.

"Do they have mirrors inside of their eyes?" Zack asked.

"I don't know," Izzy said. "I just know they have eyeshine."

"*Permíteme*," Miguel said.

"Go for it," Izzy encouraged him.

"Nocturnal animals have two things that help them see in the early morning and during *crepúsculo*," Miguel explained. "First, their eyes have more rod cells than cone cells. Rod cells need less light than cone cells, so they are very *útil* at night. Cone cells are for seeing color, so they are less *útil*—at least for nocturnal animals."

"I never knew that. That's fascinating," Mrs. Philips commented.

"Also," Miguel continued, "they have a reflector in their eye that acts as an *espejo*—a mirror—so their eyes can reflect light, allowing them to use the light twice. And because of that, we see the shine."

"Do I have a reflector in my eyes?" Zack asked.

"Are you nocturnal? Miguel asked.

"Only when he eats too much sugar," Mrs. Philips said.

Miguel laughed. "Only nocturnal animals have it—including spiders! And here is a fun thing to know: Different animals have different colors of eyeshine."

"Really?" Izzy asked.

"Of course. For us, jaguars have golden eyeshine and tapirs have red eyeshine."

"What about howler monkeys?" Izzy asked.

"They don't have it. They are diurnal monkeys. Only nocturnal monkeys have eyeshine."

"Wow, Miguel. You know so much," Zack said.

"And your English is phenomenal," Mrs. Philips added. "Did you learn it at school?"

"Thank you, Mrs. Philips. I did learn English at school, but I practice all the time with English-speaking biologists from Utah who visit Nicaragua to study birds. When I help them, we speak in English."

"I'm impressed," Mrs. Philips said. "Now, it's time for us to head home, make you something to eat, and get you settled in."

"Thank you so much, Mrs. Philips, but I'm still full from the train," he answered, patting his stomach.

"Are you sure?" Mrs. Philips asked with one eyebrow raised.

"Actually, I'm a little hungry, but I think my stomach needs to rest. I'm not used to American pizza." Miguel blushed as his stomach gurgled loudly enough for everyone to hear.

"Ah," Mrs. Philips said. "Let's get you home and I'll give you some medicine to help settle your stomach. I suspect you're also exhausted."

"Instead of medicine, can you make the drink my grandma always makes to settle my stomach?" Miguel asked.

"If I have the ingredients, I will. What does she put in it?" Mrs. Philips asked.

"She boils water with rice and then takes the water and adds garlic, lemon, and sugar. Every time I drink that, I feel better."

"Interesting. That makes a lot of sense. I can see how the rice water could help you retain water, the garlic and lemon could help kill off the germs, and the water could hydrate you, but why the sugar?"

"Can you imagine how it would taste without it?" Miguel made a face.

"Ah!" Mrs. Philips laughed.

At the house, Mrs. Philips made Miguel his grandmother's recipe and set up a cot for him in Zack's room. Zack handed him one of his stuffed animals and a book on California mammals in case he wanted to learn more about bobcats, but within minutes, Miguel was sound asleep.

3

A bobcat lurked about in the bushes. It had been hunting gophers but didn't catch any—the gophers were too fast and there was too much disruption from cars. Normally active late into the night, the exhausted bobcat laid down to rest. It stayed in the same place for over an hour without doing anything; it was even too tired to groom its matted fur. But it was also hungry and needed to find its next meal.

Finally, when the sun was down and the moon was up, the bobcat stood and sauntered over to the neighborhood next to the park to look for mice. It had been finding mice there all month, and unlike the gophers in the park, the mice moved slowly enough that the bobcat could actually catch some of them.

4

Around midnight, Miguel woke up. It was bright outside. He looked out the window, but instead of seeing a full moon, found the light was coming from a bright light attached to the Philipses' garage. It lit up the whole yard. Miguel could see a small herb garden, a wheelbarrow, a table and chairs, a shed, a huge old willow tree, and, most important to him, the bike he would borrow for the week.

Then Miguel saw a cat. *Was it the Philipses' cat*? he wondered. *No, it was too big and the Philipses keep their cat, Shadow, indoors. Could it be a bobcat right in their yard? That just didn't seem possible given that Mrs. Philips said how rare they were, but maybe it was the same one we saw at the park.*

Miguel squinted and rubbed his eyes. The

animal was moving about at the edge of the shed. It was larger than a housecat and had the short tail of a bobcat. He couldn't think of anything else it could be and wondered if it truly was the same one they'd seen at the park. It was thinner than he'd expected and was moving about more slowly than he thought a bobcat should move.

Miguel reached around for his glasses to get a better look. But by the time he got them on, the animal had disappeared around the house.

Miguel fell back to sleep, but woke again at 4am. Since his body hadn't yet adjusted to California time, his body thought it was his usual wake-up time of 6am in Nicaragua, so he was wide awake. He put on his glasses and looked out the window, hoping to see the bobcat again, but it wasn't there.

As he waited for Zack to wake up, Miguel put on his headlamp and picked up Zack's book on California mammals. He flipped past pages and pages of rabbits, rodents, and bats until he finally got to the single page on cats. *Izzy was right*, he thought, *only two kinds of wild cats live in California: mountain lions and bobcats.* He thought about the five species of wild cats that lived in Nicaragua. He knew he was lucky to have seen four of Nicaragua's cats: ocelots, margays, jaguar, and jaguarundi. But he had never seen the fifth: the puma, also known as a mountain lion, and the only cat found in both Nicaragua and California.

I want to see a puma, he thought, admiring a photo in the book showing its long, black-tipped tail. *But I do feel very lucky to have seen a bobcat.* Another photo showed a tan bobcat with its black spots, short tail, and thick, shiny coat.

Miguel read that bobcats weigh about twenty pounds, which he converted in his head to be about nine kilograms. It also said they are nocturnal and largely hunt rabbits and other small prey.

He felt sure the animal he had just seen out the window was a bobcat, but something about it wasn't right. It just didn't look as amazing as the one in the book. He spent some more time reading about bobcats and paging through the rest of the book until he heard someone up. Miguel tiptoed out of the room and down the hall to the kitchen.

There, he found Mrs. Philips sipping coffee and feeding Carson. "Hello Miguel," she greeted as he walked into the room. "How did you sleep?"

"Great—until I woke up at 4am," he answered.

"Oh . . . jet lag," Mrs. Philips said. "I suppose it will take a few days to get adjusted. How do you feel otherwise?"

"I think I'm better," Miguel said. "I think I'll just be a little tired today." Then he sniffed the air. "Your coffee smells good."

"Would you like some?"

"No thank you, but I'm glad you like coffee. My mother sent me with two bags of coffee beans for you from her *finca*. She is now the manager. It's called Finca Verde."

"*Verde*—doesn't that mean green?"

Miguel laughed. "You're right, it does. I guess

we name everything green, too. But I think you'll like it. It's very popular coffee."

"That was thoughtful of her—and how fun to drink coffee in our home that's from your home," Mrs. Philips said.

"It's also coffee that's good for the *medioambiente*. It's organic."

"Terrific. I've been trying to be better about buying organic foods—and making sure they are locally grown. I never really thought about buying organic coffee. I suppose the less pesticides we have in our bodies, the better."

"Yes, organically grown crops are good for our bodies," Miguel said, "but they are also good for the bodies of the farmworkers and the bodies of the animals using the farms as habitat."

"Oh my gosh, I've never even thought about how important organic farming is for the workers or the animals. I've only thought about how important it is for the person buying it."

"Now you can think of both," Miguel said, smiling. "And this coffee even has another benefit for the environment: it's grown in the shade. At many coffee *fincas*, the trees are cut down to increase production. Finca Verde used to do that as well. But it's bad for the birds and also for the howler monkeys that need the trees.

"My mother got the owner of Finca Verde to stop cutting trees at the same time she got him to stop using *productos químicos*—chemicals—just before I was born. It's now a beautiful place with shade for the workers and trees for the howler monkeys. It's also a chemical-free place for all."

"Your mother sounds amazing. And so does the coffee," Mrs. Philips said.

"She is. And it is. I'll go get it," Miguel said. He tiptoed back to the room and returned with two bags of coffee beans, both stamped with the logo of Finca Verde—a howler monkey sitting in a tree above a coffee plant.

"Howler monkeys. Amazing," Mrs. Philips said, shaking her head. "I would love to see a howler monkey. This is terrific. Thank you. Now, how about some waffles?"

At that, Izzy stumbled down the stairs with Zack right behind her. "Did you say waffles?" Zack said. "Can we have whipped cream on them?"

"Waffles? What are those?" Miguel asked.

"You are going to love them. They're like crunchy pancakes. We load them up with butter and maple syrup," Izzy explained.

"What's syrup? I've never had that either," Miguel said.

"Syrup is like liquid sugar. It comes from maple trees," Izzy said.

"It's *soooo* good," Zack added.

"Actually, could I please just have some tortillas? I don't want to remind my *estómago* of how it felt yesterday," Miguel asked.

"Hmmm," Mrs. Philips said. "I think that's a smart idea. Your body needs time to adjust. I don't have tortillas but how about some toast? It should be kind to your stomach."

"Thanks," he responded. "That sounds *perfecto*."

"Then I want toast, too," Zack said, sitting

down next to Miguel.

"Me three," Izzy said.

"Well, that makes things easier," Mrs. Philips said. "I'll make waffles later in the week."

"Thank you," Miguel said.

What are you kids going to do today?" Mrs. Philips asked while making the toast.

"We're going to spend the day with Brooke and Tai at the park," Izzy said.

Mrs. Philips smiled. Izzy, Zack, Tai, and Brooke were almost inseparable.

Before everyone had even taken their last bite, Izzy started cleaning up and Zack began trying to pry Miguel's soccer ball away from Carson. Sensing it was time to go, Miguel took his last bite as he brought his plate over to the sink. "Thank you for the toast, Mrs. Philips."

"You're welcome. Thank you for the coffee— and the inspiration. Do you want anything else?" she asked, but it was too late—Izzy already had the door open. Mrs. Philips shook her head and distracted Carson with some crackers so Zack

could grab the soccer ball. Then she waved as the
kids headed out the door and toward the park.

5

The Philipses used to live right next to Green County Park, but they had moved to Southern California at the end of the previous summer. There, Izzy had gone to fourth grade and Zack to kindergarten. Mrs. Philips then decided to move the family back to Greenley for the summer to be closer to their Grandma Pearl.

By then, she had sold their old house, but found a place to rent right down the street from it. That meant the rental house was also right near Brooke and Grandma Pearl's homes and in biking distance from Tai's house.

Miguel walked along with Izzy and Zack while skillfully keeping the soccer ball just ahead of him. As they approached the park, they could see two kids standing near the edge of the parking lot and waving to them. One was a girl with dark curly hair and purple glasses. The other was a tall boy wearing a cowboy hat. The boy hooted as they approached. "*Hoo-hoo-hoooo!*"

"*Hoo-hoooo!*" Miguel hooted back.

"How did you know he was hooting at us?" Zack asked.

"Who else do you think he's hooting at?" Miguel teased as he looked behind them at the empty sidewalk.

Zack laughed. "Oh, right."

"The Nature Club is finally all together!" Brooke greeted.

"Miguel, this is Brooke and Tai," Izzy said. And then to Brooke and Tai, Izzy said, "and this is my pen pal, Miguel."

Miguel gave them each a warm hug. "I'm so happy to meet you."

Tai tipped his cowboy hat. "Welcome to Green County Park, home of the Nature Club."

"I love it already. And I love your hat," Miguel said to Tai.

"And I love your glasses," Brooke said. Brooke

29

had just gotten her first pair of glasses earlier that summer and was thrilled to see that Miguel wore glasses, too.

"Thanks. And what do you think of this?" Miguel asked as he pulled off his sweatshirt to reveal his Nature Club T-shirt underneath. Brooke's dad had made one for each kid and they had mailed one to Miguel earlier that summer.

"That's so cool!" Brooke said.

Zack, who had watched Miguel pick out his shirt that morning, then pulled off his sweatshirt to show that he was also wearing his Nature Club T-shirt that day.

"Good thinking, Zack. Let's pick a day later this week to all wear them together," Izzy suggested.

"Yes! We have to before you—actually, before all three of you—disappear into the distance," Brooke said with an exaggerated sniff. For at the end of the week, Miguel was leaving, and just one week after that, Izzy and Zack would be returning to Southern California in time to start fifth and first grade.

"I can't think about that right now," Izzy said. "I'm afraid I'll cry."

"It doesn't matter where you are, we will always be best friends forever," Brooke said, linking her pinky around Izzy's. "Pinky promise."

"Pinky promise," Izzy repeated quietly.

"Izzy says you're one master soccer player," Tai said to Miguel, trying to lighten the mood. "How 'bout you teach us some tricks? Brooke plays softball and us three do karate, but we're not too good at soccer."

"Great," Miguel answered. "I love soccer, except we call it *futbol* in Nicaragua."

"Is it popular in Nicaragua?" Brooke asked.

"Actually, you would fit in great in Nicaragua because baseball is the most popular sport, but I just love soccer," Miguel answered. He then kicked the ball into the air, juggled it back and forth on his knees, and passed it to Zack.

"How 'bout a game?" Tai suggested. "That field's public," Tai said, pointing to an empty lot next to the park. "Let's play there."

"Great idea!" Brooke said.

"Well then, *juguemos*!" Miguel said and passed the ball to Brooke.

"How are we going to play a game with only five people?" Izzy asked.

"Easy," Miguel joked. "The four of us will play against you."

"Right," Izzy said, with her hands on her hips.

"How about us against them?" Zack suggested to Miguel.

"You got it," Miguel answered.

The kids used their sweatshirts and Zack's stuffed penguin to mark goals and played until Izzy, Brooke, and Tai were ready for a break. To no one's great surprise, Miguel and Zack won, but they all had a great time.

While the others rested, Zack asked Miguel to teach him how to do a goalie kick. Miguel showed Zack how to toss the ball into the air and then kick it far into the distance by demonstrating and having Zack retrieve the ball. Then it was Zack's turn. Zack missed the first three times. Then he kicked the ball far and high, but way off to the side. It went right out of the field and into the yard of the house next door. It rolled and then disappeared into a shed.

"*No te preocupes*, I'll get it," Miguel yelled and ran to the shed.

The ball had rolled far enough inside that Miguel had to enter the shed to retrieve it. Inside, the shed was packed with gardening tools, snow shovels, and even old bikes. *This is the shed of a busy person*, Miguel thought. Then he bent down to retrieve the ball and came face to face with a shelf full of poisons.

He scanned the labels: insecticides, herbicides, rodenticides. *There must be at least ten boxes and bottles of poison in here*, Miguel thought. "Why?" he said out loud. "Why do adults have to poison the Earth?" Then he grabbed the ball and left to join the others.

The others were standing in a circle and talking excitedly.

"You saw a bobcat?" Miguel could hear Brooke

saying to Izzy as he approached the group. "You are so lucky! I've never seen one and I've lived here all my life! I can't believe it took you all day to tell us."

"I think I just got distracted with all of us being together for the first time," Izzy said.

"And with me and Miguel winning at soccer," Zack added with a big smile.

"Ah! The bobcat," Miguel said as he rejoined the group. "I have more news . . . I forgot to tell even Izzy. I saw it again late last night."

"What?" Izzy said.

"I woke up around *medianoche* and looked out the window. I saw the bobcat by the shed—or at least *some* bobcat. I'm sure of it. I looked it up in Zack's book. I watched it walk across the yard. I grabbed my glasses for a better look, but it had already disappeared."

"You've already seen a bobcat *twice* and you just got here yesterday?" Brooke said. "Wow. I'm going to stick with you."

"The thing was, when I saw it again last night,

it didn't look quite right. It looked sick and it seemed slow," Miguel said.

"Maybe it was tired from being up at night," Zack said.

"Zack, it's nocturnal," Izzy said.

"Oh. Right."

"Speaking of tired and sick, I still feel a little weird. My stomach keeps gurgling and I feel like I need some sleep. Do you mind if we head back?"

"I need to get rolling, too," Tai said. "Time to feed Dune." Dune was Tai's horse and even though Dune grazed in his pasture, Tai liked spoiling him with handfuls of sweet hay.

"Before we all head off, let's do our five-minute litter pickup," Izzy said.

"Sounds good," Tai said. "Then we will have shown Miguel a real Nature Club day at our favorite place!"

The kids talked a little more about the bobcat while picking up litter.

"Miguel, we sure are glad you're here," Tai said.

"*Gracias amigo*. I'm so happy to be here, too."

"Well, I better go. See ya tomorrow, friends," Tai yelled as he jumped on his bike and pedaled into the distance.

The others waved until Tai was out of sight and then walked home. Before Brooke split off, she made Miguel promise to send the bobcat over to her house if he saw it again. They all laughed and headed home for dinner.

6

"We're home!" Izzy called to her mom as they walked into the house.

"Oh, great. Can you watch Carson while I make dinner?" Mrs. Philips asked while Carson waddled up to them.

"I will," Miguel offered. "I love little kids."

"But he's so sticky," Zack said, making a face.

Miguel looked at Zack's filthy feet, his dirty red hair standing on end, his cast covered in grease stains, and the holes in his clothes. Even Otto the penguin was dirty. "Good point," Miguel laughed, shaking his head.

"How about if you all wash your hands while I wash Carson and *then* you watch him for me?" Mrs. Philips suggested. "Besides, while I'm glad Miguel is feeling better, it never hurts to keep the germs away."

After they cleaned up, Miguel played with Carson while Izzy and Zack helped their mom make dinner and set the table. Then they all sat down together to enjoy soup, salad, and homemade bread.

"This soup is *deliciosa*," Miguel said.

"Thank you. I made it because I thought you could use some salty fluids to finish settling your stomach. It will also help hydrate you."

"Thank you for thinking of me," Miguel said.

"Well, thank you for that coffee. I made a cup of it this afternoon and it was really very good."

Miguel smiled. "My mom grows good coffee." Then Miguel grew somewhat thoughtful. "Mrs. Philips, can I call my mom?" he asked.

"Of course. Here, you can use my phone. Do you have her number?"

"Yes. Thank you."

Miguel took the phone, stepped outside, and called his parents' hotel room.

"*Hola*," his mother answered.

"*Mamá, es Miguel*," he said.

"*Aja Mijo. ¿Como está todo?*" she asked.

Miguel told her all about the park, the other kids, their house, and finally, about the bobcat.

His mother told him about the conference, the hotel, and how they were serving Finca Verde's coffee at the hotel restaurant.

Miguel told his mother that Mrs. Philips liked the coffee and was excited to learn about the howler monkeys. "Maybe you should start your talk with a picture of howler monkeys," he suggested.

"Oh, my talk. I'm very nervous," she said.

"But you give talks all the time," Miguel said.

"But this might be a very big crowd," she said. "Or maybe not. What if nobody comes?"

"They will come! And you will give a great talk. And you will make a difference. Someday, I want to make a difference in the world like you," Miguel said.

"You always make a difference in *my* world," his mother responded. "Now you need to get some sleep. Please tell Mrs. Philips I said hello."

"I will," he promised

"*Te amo, Chavalo*," she said.

"*Te amo, Mamá*," he responded.

Señora Ramirez then handed the phone to her husband so he could talk with Miguel.

After Miguel hung up with his parents, he said good night to the others and got ready for bed. He laid down and fell asleep immediately, but just like the night before, woke in the night. *At least I might see that bobcat again*, he thought. He put on his glasses and watched out the window for half an hour but didn't see anything.

He considered giving up watching when some mice appeared from around the shed. Like the bobcat the night before, they moved slowly. Suddenly, the bobcat appeared and pounced on one of the mice. Or at least *tried* to pounce. *That was a pretty lame pounce*, Miguel thought. It missed the mouse, but then caught a different one and sat down to eat it. This time, because of the spotlight, Miguel got a good look.

The bobcat wasn't just thin, it was also

scraggly looking. Its hair looked matted and dingy, and one of its ears was ripped and bleeding. When the bobcat finished its meal and stood up to walk away, it moved slowly and even wobbled. Miguel watched as it crossed the yard and disappeared around the shed.

Miguel then laid down, grateful his own sickness seemed so mild in comparison, and fell back to sleep.

7

The bobcat stumbled around a shed and out into a brightly lit yard, looking for mice. Occasionally, one would run past, and the bobcat would lope after it. Luckily for the bobcat, the mice were slow and wobbly.

The bobcat missed the first mouse but grabbed the second one by the tail. The bobcat ate that one and then caught three more. It quickly devoured their meager bodies. Due to the bobcat's weakened state, that was enough to eat for one night.

It wove back around the shed and tried to jump a small fence to drink from the neighbor's birdbath. It made the jump, but then stumbled and fell back into the fence and re-injured a tear on its right ear. It hardly seemed to notice. The bobcat was already filthy and tattered, and riddled with cuts and sores. This injury was just one more discomfort.

The bobcat stood and slowly made its way back to the park. It sat down under a bush and started to groom its fur, but when dizziness took over, it instead put its head down, closed its eyes, and fell into a restless sleep.

8

When Miguel woke up, it was light out, and everyone else was already up. Being awake in the middle of the night had tired him out, and he'd ended up sleeping in until 7am. He entered the kitchen with energy and a smile.

"You look terrific," Mrs. Philips said. "Are you feeling better?"

"I am. I think my body has adjusted to the time difference and the food. I feel *mucho mejor*."

"You must have slept deeply if Zack didn't wake you up this morning," Mrs. Philips said.

"I sure did. But it's partly because I was up late. And guess what I saw again?"

"You saw the bobcat again?" Izzy asked.

"I sure did. Unfortunately, it looked sick. It moved slowly and it looked . . . what's the word? Scraggly?"

"Hmmm . . . that doesn't sound right at all," Mrs. Philips said.

"We have to help it," Zack said.

"How sick do you think it was?" Izzy asked.

"I don't know. I wish I could've gotten a closer look, but I could tell that its fur was patchy, and it seemed . . . wobbly," Miguel said.

"Can we leave out that rice-water and garlic potion you made for Miguel?" Zack asked.

"We can't feed wild animals," Izzy said. "Don't you remember what Victoria said?"

"Who's Victoria?" Miguel asked.

Izzy explained that Victoria was a wildlife biologist who worked for the county. Earlier that summer, she had taught them how damaging it is to let wild animals get human food or garbage. She had told them that the animals get used to it and end up hanging around developed areas to try and get more.

"Once that happens," she said, "they get into conflicts with humans and sometimes get hit by cars since developed areas are near roads."

"Well, what are we going to do?" Zack asked.

"It's hard to know what to do unless we know what's wrong with it," Miguel said.

"Then let's try to find it and get a better look," Izzy said.

"Oh Izzy, you know how secretive they are," Mrs. Philips said.

"Yeah, but Miguel has already seen one bobcat three times," Izzy said.

"Or he's seen three bobcats once," Zack added.

"Hmm. I guess you're right," Mrs. Philips said. But if you find it, don't get too close, okay? Wild animals can be unpredictable when they're sick."

"We won't, Mom. Don't forget—Victoria also taught us to never approach wild animals even when they're healthy so they don't get—what was the word?" Izzy asked.

"Habituated," Mrs. Philips said.

"Right, habituated."

Just then, the doorbell rang. Brooke and Tai were there. They had just come from the park, where they had seen the bobcat under a bush.

"Really? Miguel saw it here again last night, too," Izzy said.

"Sorry I didn't send it over to your house," Miguel said to Brooke with a smile.

Brooke laughed. "Well, I got a good look at it today, but it wasn't the beautiful, wild bobcat I was hoping to see. It just didn't look healthy. Its fur was all matted and it looked thin. It also had a big cut on its right ear."

"I bet it's the same one," Miguel said. "I also got a better look at a bobcat last night and when it walked, it seemed like it was wobbling—and it also had a cut on its ear."

"What are we going to do?" Zack asked, tugging on Izzy's shirt. "We have to do something."

"How 'bout we call Victoria?" Tai suggested.

"Good idea," Brooke said. "She'll know what to do to help it."

"Here, let me get her number for you," Mrs. Philips said. She looked it up on her cell phone, dialed, and handed the phone to Izzy.

"Hello, Green County wildlife, how can I help you?" Victoria answered.

"Hi Victoria, it's Izzy from the Nature Club."

"Hi Izzy, how are you doing?" Victoria asked warmly.

"I'm good, but a local bobcat isn't. My friend Miguel has seen it three nights in a row and said it looked sick. Then today, Tai and Brooke saw it lying under a bush at the park and said it looked thin and its fur was patchy. We think we are all seeing the same bobcat because of a cut in its right ear."

"I'm glad you called," Victoria said. "I've had a few other reports of a sick bobcat. I'll be right out. Why don't you kids meet me at the park?"

"Great, see you in a few minutes," Izzy said.

"Okay," Victoria responded and they hung up.

"We need to meet Victoria at the park right away," Izzy said.

"Good luck," Mrs. Philips said, pulling Carson onto her lap.

48

9

Within minutes, Izzy, Zack, Tai, Brooke, and Miguel were out the door and heading down the street to the park. As they walked, they chatted excitedly about what Victoria would do and told Miguel about the time they got to help her catch a family of bears in a culvert trap.

Almost immediately after they arrived, Victoria pulled her truck into the gravel lot. She grabbed her binoculars, jumped out of the truck, and greeted the kids.

"Hi there," she said, followed quickly by, "Oh, there it is . . . everyone, stay with me and be very still and quiet."

Victoria crouched down behind a bush and watched the bobcat through her binoculars. It was lying under a bush about fifty yards away. As the group watched, it occasionally stood, wobbled around for a bit, and then sat back down. When it turned its head, they could see the tear in its right ear.

"Wow. It really does look rough," Victoria said. "Its fur is patchy and matted."

After she got a good look at it, she passed the binoculars to the others to take a look.

"I'm afraid this cat is sick," Victoria said. "I'm going to catch it and take it to Ruby."

"Who's Ruby?" Brooke asked.

"Ruby is the local wildlife rehabilitator," Victoria answered. "Haven't you kids met her?"

They all shook their heads from side to side.

"She's terrific. She was a veterinarian in Australia and moved to California after she retired. Then she opened up a rehabilitation center for raptors and small to mid-sized mammals. Whenever I find wild animals with injuries, I bring them to her. She brings them back to health and releases them."

"I thought you said not to take wild animals into captivity," Zack said quietly.

"You're right. Let me clarify. When I find a wild animal with injuries caused by human negligence that can be saved, I take it to Ruby."

"Aren't you afraid they will catch diseases from other animals at the rehabilitation center and then spread the disease to other wildlife when they are released?" Izzy asked.

"You kids catch on quickly," Victoria said. "That's an excellent question. If there's a chance one animal could get a disease from another animal in the rehab center, we have a veterinarian look at it before we release it. We only release an animal if and when the vet gives us the okay. Since Ruby's a vet, it's one-stop shopping."

Victoria put on a thick jacket, goggles, and leather gloves. Then she leaned into the back of her truck and grabbed a metal pole. It had rubber grips on it and a loop of cable sticking out the top.

"What's that?" Brooke asked.

"This is a catch pole. This bobcat is moving so slowly that I think I can just grab it with this pole and then transfer it into a transport cage to take it to the rehab center. Now, you kids, please stay back. Sick animals can act unpredictably and can carry diseases that you don't want."

They all nodded quietly. Victoria moved slowly toward the bobcat. The bobcat lifted its head to look at her, but then lay its head back down. Victoria easily grabbed it, transferred it to the other cage and lifted that cage into the back of her truck.

"Wow, look at that poor thing," Brooke said.

"That bobcat does not look one bit healthy," Tai said.

"It's such a beautiful animal," Miguel said. "I sure hope Ruby can help it."

"Me too," Victoria said. "This bobcat clearly needs care. I think it also needs a lot of luck."

"Don't you worry, I've got my lucky penny," Tai said. He took it out of his pocket and flipped it into the air. He caught it with his right hand and slapped it down onto the back of his left hand. Then he looked at it and stuffed it back into his pocket. "Tails. Tails never fails," Tai said. "That cat's gonna be just fine."

"That is good solid science," Miguel said with a wink and a smile.

"Hey, whatever works," Tai said, patting the pocket where he kept the penny.

"If you can, come by tomorrow and visit Ruby's place. I'm sure she'd love to show you around."

"Where's Ruby's place?" Izzy asked.

"Right behind the Clementine Inn," Victoria said and got into her truck. "I gotta get going. Good work, team!" she called out the window as she drove off.

"Clementine," Miguel said.

"Right. The Clementine Inn," Izzy said.

"You know what, I like that name," Miguel said. "Let's name him Clementine."

"Who?" Zack asked.

"The bobcat!" Brooke said, laughing.

"Isn't that a girl's name?" Tai asked.

"I don't think names have genders anymore," Brooke said.

"Hmm," Tai said. "Let me think on that."

"If you don't like Clementine, you can always call him 'Clem'," Brooke suggested.

"Still thinking," Tai said.

"While you think, how about we play some soccer?" Miguel said as he juggled the ball from foot to foot and then passed it to Brooke.

The kids played soccer until they needed a water break.

"I've got a treat for us," Brooke said. "I brought some juice my dad bought last week. Want to have one before we head home?"

"That'd be great," Miguel said. "I could use a little sugar boost."

Brooke passed the bottles around.

"We don't have this kind of juice where I live," Miguel said. "Although there are lots of bottles of other drinks, including lots of soda."

"Really? Here we have so many choices of what to drink that it's almost crazy," Izzy said.

"And you also have more recycling here. We don't have recycling in my town, so I never buy bottled drinks—even though our water isn't always great. You are so lucky you have a choice of drinking good tap water *or* buying drinks and recycling the bottles," Miguel said.

"We are. But I'd rather have howler monkeys," Brooke said. "Monkeys are so cool."

"You've got a lot of cool things here. There's so much to see. I'm so anxious to write in my journal and do some drawings," Miguel said.

"How about we meet here in the morning and do some journaling before going to Ruby's?" Brooke suggested.

"Great idea," Tai said. "But right now, it's time to head on home."

The kids got up and stretched and then spent five minutes picking up litter. When they were done, they all headed home.

When Izzy, Zack, and Miguel got back to the Philipses' house, Miguel again entertained Carson while the others helped their mom with dinner. After dinner, they all got into their pajamas and had a lively discussion about whether names had genders until they were tired.

Miguel then made a quick call to his parents, got ready for bed, fell asleep easily, and dreamed about Clementine.

10

The next morning, the Nature Club assembled at the park early so they could spend a half hour sketching and journaling before biking out to the rehab center. It was a perfect day, so thirty minutes stretched into almost an hour before Zack asked, "Can we go see Clem now?"

They got on their bikes and rode along the path to the Clementine Inn. When they got to the inn, they saw a sign next to it that said, "Ruby's Rehab" with an arrow pointing down a dirt road.

They followed the dirt road around the back of the inn and got to a small wooden house with a crooked porch out front. They walked up the front steps and found a sign on the door that said, "All creatures are welcome here."

They knocked on the door, but no one answered, so they went around to the back. It was a different world back there—almost like walking into a tiny zoo. There were huge cages set up with a variety of animals in them and then one enormous cage with a hawk inside.

"I want a yard like this," Zack said to Izzy.

Before she could respond, they heard, "G'day!" from a voice with a distinctive accent well before they saw anyone.

"Hello!" Brooke yelled back toward the voice. "It's us. We're here—behind the house."

"Hello us," a woman with bright pink cheeks and gray hair pulled up in a bun said to them as she walked up. "You must be the kids from the Nature Club."

"Yes. That's us. I mean, that's who we are," Izzy said blushing.

"Glad you could come! I'm Ruby. I reckon you're keen to see the bobcat?"

"We are!" they all said at once.

"Right this way," Ruby said and led them down a path to a large cage within which they found the bobcat.

"How is Clementine?" Miguel asked.

"You mean Clem," Tai said.

"Who's Clem?" Ruby asked.

"Clem is the bobcat," Zack said.

"Oh, you named her? She's doing just great," Ruby said.

"Clementine's a girl?" Tai asked.

"Indeed she is," Ruby said smiling at them.

Brooke elbowed Tai and whispered, "But you can still call her Clem."

"Will Clementine be okay?" Miguel asked.

"She is. But she's pretty sick and will need to stay here for a few weeks—maybe more," Ruby said. "She definitely has mange, that's for sure, but I think she's also been poisoned with rat poison. She has lots of the symptoms: she had a bloody nose, she's thin and shaky, and she's very dehydrated. I've sent blood samples to a lab to find out for certain."

"Rat poison? Why would anyone give her rat poison?" Brooke asked.

"I think it was a case of secondary poisoning.

In other words, someone probably used it on mice or rats or gophers. Then she probably ate one of the rodents and got sick. Then once she got sick, she got more susceptible to mange. I've seen it heaps around here.

"The cut on her ear is also probably related. She may have been stumbling around and got hurt on something. There's also more blood dried in her fur than there should be. Rat poison makes it harder for blood to clot so the animal bleeds more than usual."

"I thought bobcats were hunters, not scavengers," Izzy said. "Why would she eat a dead rodent?"

"It takes several days for the rodents to die after they're poisoned. While they're sick, they'll still be out and about looking for food and water, but they'll be moving slowly—so they're a cinch for bobcats and other predators to catch."

"I saw some poison in the shed at one of the houses next to the park," Miguel said. "I saw it when the soccer ball rolled into it the other day."

"It's bonkers what people do to get rid of rodents," Ruby said, shaking her head. "It's cruel to the rodents *and* cruel to the rodents' predators. I've seen snakes, hawks, owls, and bobcats all get horribly sick from rat poison. The irony is that they're nature's rodent control—but they can't do their job if they're poisoned."

"That's horrible," Izzy said.

"Why does anyone use rat poison when it's so awful?" Brooke asked.

"People forget we live in a connected world. They get focused. They get busy. They don't know. Lots of reasons—but none of them good," Ruby said. "You know, some people believe we each have a circle of influence and beyond that, there isn't much we can do."

"I get that. I wish I had more influence to make a difference," Miguel said.

"My mom says the circle is more like a balloon of influence and that if we blow a little more air in the balloon, our influence grows," Izzy said.

"Hmm. I don't buy it. I think we each have the

61

chance to have lots of influence. Do you know why?" Ruby asked.

The kids all shook their heads.

"Because we're all interconnected. You can think of it as a web or a network or a matrix or whatever you want, but the main thing to remember is that we're in this game together and what we do—or don't do—matters."

"What game?" Miguel asked.

Ruby smiled, "The game of life, mate."

"I don't get it," Zack said.

"Hmm. Can one of you give an example of an impact you've had on others? It can be intentional or unintentional," Ruby asked.

"I can give an example of an impact my mom's had," Miguel offered.

"Beauty. Let's hear it," Ruby said.

"My mom has helped birds and howler monkeys," Miguel replied. "Before I was born, she got the owner of the coffee farm where she works to stop cutting down trees and using chemicals. Now lots of birds and howler monkeys live there."

"That's brilliant," Ruby said. "How'd she do it?

"She got sick from the pesticides and talked to her boss about it. He'd been sick, too. They decided to switch to organic and their company made more money. It turned out people wanted to support a company that cares about the *medioambiente*."

"Good on her," Ruby said. "She sounds like an amazing woman."

"She is!" Miguel beamed. "She's now the manager of the *finca*."

"But if you live in Nicaragua, what are you doing here?"

"My parents are attending a conference in San Francisco and they brought me to visit my pen pal, Izzy," Miguel said.

"How wonderful!" Ruby said. "What type of conference?"

"It's all about growing organic coffee. My mom is giving the closing speech at the banquet tomorrow night!" Miguel said.

"Oh, that's terrific," Ruby said. "I reckon she'll

have a massive impact."

"My mom is worried that no one will come and she won't have an impact, but I think she will. I wish we could have an impact, too," Miguel said.

"Maybe we *can* have some impact to help animals like Clementine," Izzy said.

"There has to be something the Nature Club can do to stop the poisoning," Brooke said.

"That would be terrific. I don't mind having such a nice houseguest as Clem here, but I hate seeing how she's suffering," Ruby said.

"It's so awful that she's sick. By the way, what exactly is mange?" Brooke asked.

"Mange is a condition that happens when mites burrow into skin and then live in there."

"Oh no. You did not just say mites are living in Clem's skin. That is so gross," Brooke said.

Ruby laughed. "It is gross, but honestly, we have heaps of microbes living on us.

"I'm going to throw up," Brooke said.

"Come on, Brooke. Haven't you ever had lice?" Tai asked.

Brooke's expression of disgust got everyone laughing.

"So, what do the mites do to the bobcats?" Miguel asked.

"The mites cause their animal hosts to lose their hair and get thick, cracked skin," Ruby explained. "Between that and all the bacteria the mites bring, the host animals then often get infections. Because of the infections, the animals become weak, thin, and dehydrated, and they can eventually die."

Zack had a look of horror on his face. "You can help Clementine, right?"

"I'll do my best. I've already given her some vitamin K injections and am now working on getting her hydrated and letting her rest."

"What's the vitamin K for?" Brooke asked.

"Rat poison inhibits vitamin K from doing its job of forming the proteins needed to clot blood. I reckon that's why she had a bloody nose."

"Oh . . . will she be better by tomorrow?" Brooke asked.

"She'll be on the mend . . . ," Ruby said.

"I told you," Tai said while patting the pocket with his lucky penny.

"That's a relief!" Brooke said with a sigh.

". . . but it won't be by tomorrow," Ruby said. "It might take a month or more. She's really sick. But I'll keep her safe while she recovers. When animals are sick like this, they are so vulnerable— they even get hit more often by cars."

The kids all thanked Ruby and asked her to keep them updated. She promised she would and thanked them for their good work. Then they hopped on their bikes and headed home.

11

As the kids rode home, Tai suggested they all stop by his house so Miguel could meet his dad.

When they got there, Tai's horse, Dune, was standing right near the front fence.

"What a beautiful horse," Miguel said.

"Want to ride him?" Tai asked.

"*Absolutamente!*" Miguel answered.

In no time, Miguel was up in the saddle and circling the pasture. After one round, Tai tossed Miguel his cowboy hat, which Miguel caught and set jauntily on his head.

"Watch this," Miguel said and set off across the pasture. He and Dune did a few laps and the second time he passed Tai, he tossed the hat back onto Tai's head.

"You're a natural," Tai hollered across the pasture.

Mr. Davis, a mustached man with a cowboy hat like his son, had been watching from the porch. He yelled, "Nice!" and walked over to join the group. Miguel rode up and dismounted to meet him.

"You must be Miguel," Mr. Davis said. "I'm Tai's dad, Mr. Davis. *Bienvenidos!*"

"Oh, thank you, Mr. Davis. *Mucho gusto.*"

"You're a great rider. Tai tells me you're also a soccer pro and most importantly," Mr. Davis winked, "a good birder."

Miguel looked over at Tai and smiled, "I suppose I'm not too bad."

"Are you having a good visit?" Mr. Davis asked.

"Yes, a great visit. I love the park and it's so good to be with my friends," Miguel answered. He also told Mr. Davis about the bobcat.

"Yes, Tai told me. Rat poison is really bad stuff," Mr. Davis said shaking his head. "It's an awful death for the rodents and it poisons thousands of pets and predators every year. Even human children get poisoned."

"Humans eat the poisoned rats and mice?" Brooke asked with a look of disgust.

Mr. Davis laughed. "No, they don't eat the rats. Little kids sample their environment by putting things in their mouths. When they come across the poison and don't know what it is—they put it in their mouth."

"Ugh. That's horrible," Izzy said.

"Yes, it is," Mr. Davis agreed. "Come on. I want to show you the rodent-control method I use."

Mr. Davis motioned for the kids to follow him. They walked across the pasture to a tall metal pole with a large wooden box mounted near the top of it. It had an elliptical opening in the front.

"An owl box?" Miguel asked.

"You got it. It's a barn owl box," Mr. Davis answered as he looked at the ground. Then he leaned over and picked up what looked like a dark, cylindrical clump of dirt.

"Ahh. An owl pellet!" Miguel said.

"Is that owl poop?" Zack asked.

"Nope," Mr. Davis answered. "Owls can't chew

69

their food so they swallow it whole. They then digest the parts they can and regurgitate the parts they can't. This pellet is the product of that regurgitation."

"Regurgitate? As in puke?" Zack asked.

"Zack!" Izzy scolded.

"It's okay," Mr. Davis said. "Owls actually are puking when they regurgitate up pellets."

"And you touched it?" Brooke asked.

"Luckily, owl puke is very different from human puke. Owls have a first stomach that's like ours in that it mixes the food with acids and liquifies it. That's the stomach our puke comes from. But owls then have a second stomach called a gizzard. The gizzard grinds down the remaining hard parts. It sends all the digestible food into the intestines and then squeezes the remaining indigestible parts like skulls, claws, and feathers into a pellet like this one."

"Do all birds puke up pellets?" Zack asked. Izzy glared at him. "What I mean is, do all birds regurgitate pellets?"

"Only owls," Mr. Davis answered. "Other birds have an organ called a crop that allows them to store and then slowly digest the parts that would be indigestible to an owl."

"Anyway, check this out," he said while breaking the pellet apart. The kids gathered around Mr. Davis while he showed them tiny bits of bones and feathers in the pellet. There was even an intact gopher skull.

"That skull is too cute!" Brooke said.

"It's amazing," Zack added.

"Oh . . . I get it," Brooke said. "The owl eats the rodents so you don't even need rat poison."

"Exactly," Mr. Davis said. "In this pasture, the owls keep the gophers under control. They get a meal and Dune gets a smoother pasture. It's a win-win. Plus, who wouldn't want a family of owls nearby? Owls make the best neighbors."

"I would like it," Miguel said.

"What a great idea. An apartment for owls," Brooke said.

"Do you worry about predators finding them

and eating them?" Izzy asked.

"I do. Especially raccoons. That's why it's up on this high metal pole. Also, do you see that metal pan thing?"

The kids all looked up and nodded.

"Well, that's used to keep any predators that can climb the pole from getting to the box."

"It must be working since you have pellets," Miguel observed, "but have they raised young?"

"I put the box up in February and barn owls already fledged three young from it."

"That's so cool," Zack said.

"Wait," Brooke said. "I thought owls nested in trees. Can't they find their own homes?"

"That's an excellent question," Mr. Davis said. "In a natural environment, they can, but since we're in an urban area where a lot of trees have been cut down, owls need options."

"This is all starting to make sense," Izzy said.

"What's making sense?" Miguel asked.

"The reason people near the park are using rat poison," she said.

"I'm not following you . . . at all," Tai said.

"My mom said the year we moved here, a lot of trees around Green County Park blew down in a giant storm," Izzy said. "If owls lost places to nest, they may have gone somewhere else, and then . . ."

"And then there would be *menos* natural predators to eat the rodents so the people turned to rat poison!" Miguel finished for her.

"County records do show fewer barn owls in recent years than a decade ago," Mr. Davis said.

"Oh no!" We need to build more owl boxes right away," Brooke said.

"Yes! That's a perfect job for the Nature Club," Izzy agreed. "And it's perfect that we have a Nature Club project while Miguel is here."

"How 'bout it, Dad? Can you help?" Tai asked.

"I'd love to help," Mr. Davis answered. "I'm off work tomorrow. How about if we meet here tomorrow at ten in the morning? We can sketch out a plan, get what we need at the hardware store, and build the boxes after lunch."

"Any chance there'll be time to ride Dune in there somewhere?" Miguel asked.

"Absolutely," Mr. Davis said. "Dune wouldn't have it any other way."

All the kids laughed when they realized Dune had been head-butting Miguel the whole time, trying to get him out for another ride. Miguel obliged until it was time to head home.

Before bed, Miguel borrowed Mrs. Philips's phone to make a quick call to his parents. He excitedly told them about how the Nature Club had found a way to make a difference—at least locally. After the call, he fell sound asleep.

12

The next morning, when the kids showed up at Tai's house, Mr. Davis had already set out his tools and a pile of scrap wood.

"This is cool," Miguel said as he eyed Mr. Davis's array of tools.

"Yes, we are going to have fun," Mr. Davis said. "Now, I called the county office already this morning and talked to Janet Helling to find out if we need any permits."

"What'd she say?" Brooke asked.

"She said that if we donate the boxes to the county, they will take care of any paperwork and install them for us."

"So what'd you say?" Brooke asked.

"I said she had herself a deal!" Mr. Davis answered.

"Where's she going to put them?" Izzy asked.

"How about our yard?" Zack suggested.

Mr. Davis laughed. "Wouldn't that be fun?" Everyone nodded. "Actually, she will put them around the edge of town where they're far from lights and noise and close to foraging areas. She's also going to make sure they aren't installed right near the bigger roads—we don't want any owls hit by cars while foraging for mice."

"Darn. I wanted one in our yard," Zack said.

"How about a bat box?" Mr. Davis suggested. "A bat box would be fine in your yard."

"But the vast majority of bats don't eat rodents," Izzy said.

"You're right. Here in California, all the bats eat insects," Mr. Davis said.

"How are insect-eating bats going to help with the rodent problem?" Brooke asked.

"They won't help with the goal of controlling rodents, but they will help with the goal of reducing people's use of chemicals. When bats eat insects, people use less insecticides," Mr. Davis explained.

"Oh, I get it!" Brooke said. "Can we make one for my yard, too?"

"And Grandma Pearl's yard?" Izzy added.

"And don't forget about us," Tai said.

"Not me," Miguel said. "I can't carry one on the plane, but I'll make one when I get home. In Nicaragua, we have ninety-four species of bats and I'm sure at least one of them will like it—at least one of the smaller species."

"That's fantastic diversity," Mr. Davis said.

"It is. We have insect-eating bats that keep down the bugs, fruit-eating bats that disperse seeds, and even nectar-feeding bats that are important pollinators," Miguel said.

"Amazing. I would love to visit your country one day," Mr. Davis said thoughtfully.

"You are welcome at my house anytime," Miguel said. Then he smiled and added, "Except today. Today we need to make some boxes."

"Right," Mr. Davis said, snapping out of his daydream. "We need to make four bat boxes. And how many owl boxes should we make?"

"We probably need about a hundred," Zack answered.

Mr. Davis laughed, saying, "That seems a bit high. How about if we make three?"

"Only three?" Zack said.

"That's actually quite a bit of work for one day," Mr. Davis answered.

"Right. Barn owl territories are probably so big that only three would fit in our town," Izzy said.

"Actually," Mr. Davis said, "unlike other owls, barn owls aren't territorial. They will even nest right next to each other. However, they still cover a lot of area, so three will be plenty.

"Okay, let's get started. We can use the pattern I used to make my barn owl box, or we can find a new one."

"Where would we go to find a new one?" Miguel asked.

"The internet, of course. The place we find everything these days," Mr. Davis said.

"I like the one you made. Can we use that pattern?" Brooke said. "It's so symmetrical."

"That would be the easiest. It also means we don't have to go to the store, as I have enough scrap material to make them, plus the bat boxes. Does that sound good?" Mr. Davis asked.

"It sounds terrific," Miguel said as the others nodded in agreement.

The group immediately got to work measuring and cutting the wood. By the time they stopped for lunch, they had all the parts cut and sanded. Mr. Davis went inside to make everyone sandwiches while the kids relaxed and Miguel took a ride on Dune. When Mr. Davis returned, they all sat in the shade and had a picnic together.

"In just a few hours, there won't be any more rat poison in Greenley," Zack said.

"Unfortunately, it doesn't work quite that fast," Mr. Davis said. "We'll install the boxes today, but it won't be until next year that the owls will find them and start nesting in them."

"Oh," Zack said looking down. Then he brightened up again, saying, "but by next year, there won't be any more poison."

"If only it were that easy," Mr. Davis said.

"What do you mean, Mr. Davis?" Brooke asked. "Won't the owls take care of the mice and gophers?"

"And then no one will need to use rat poison," Zack added.

"Well no one actually *needs* rat poison," Miguel pointed out.

"Seriously!" Izzy said. "But less people will even *want* rat poison, right?"

"Right," Mr. Davis said. "At least not for outside their homes. But people also use rat poison to control rodents inside their homes. In fact, that's where pets usually get into it. That's also where kids usually get into it."

"That's just horrible," Izzy said thinking of her cat, Shadow, and her little brother, Carson. "What's the solution?" Izzy asked.

"An owl door to let owls inside?" Zack asked.

Mr. Davis smiled. "Good idea. But, here's the thing. We want to keep wildlife outside. That means keeping out the predators, but it also means keeping out the prey—in other words, the rodents. And we do that through exclusion."

"Exclusion? We aren't allowed to do that at school. We have to let everyone eat together at lunch," Zack said.

"Right. It isn't nice to exclude others. But in this instance, it's okay. If we don't let rodents in our homes, we don't have a desire to kill them."

"That sounds like a good trade-off to me!" Brooke said.

"How do we do it?" Tai asked.

"There are two basic things we need to do. For one, we need to make our houses less attractive to rodents," Mr. Davis said.

"How?" Brooke asked.

"Get rid of the attractants," Mr. Davis said. "Sweep or vacuum regularly. Clean up right after meals. Put lids on the garbage cans. Pull out appliances and clean behind them."

"I remember when we were getting ready to move last fall and my mom pulled out the refrigerator," Izzy said. "It was so . . ."

"Gross," Zack finished for her.

"What's the second thing?" Miguel asked.

"We need to make it impossible—or at least difficult—for rodents to enter. That means closing up all gaps over one-quarter of an inch."

"That's only about six and a half millimeters," Miguel calculated in his head. "That's tiny! Is that even possible?"

"It is if you're creative and know where to look," Mr. Davis explained. "The biggest sources of entry are under doors, around windows, and under sinks. For the doors, we install these pieces of metal called door sweeps to close the gap. To close up the gaps around plumbing, we can use steel wool. You just jam it in the cracks and then line it with caulking."

"That doesn't sound too hard," Miguel said.

"Right, but the problem is, people don't do it," Mr. Davis said. "Poisons are just so available that people turn to them, thinking they are the easiest solution."

"I wish we could get the whole neighborhood

to exclude rodents," Brooke said.

"I don't know about the whole neighborhood, but how about if we start with our own homes?" Izzy asked.

"Great idea," Mr. Davis said. "There's still time today. Let's head over to the hardware store, get supplies, and then get to work."

13

Everyone biked to the hardware store together. Miguel carried Zack's stuffed penguin, Otto, since Zack was already riding with just one arm due to his cast. Miguel laughed as he carried Otto, but he laughed even harder when they arrived at the store and he saw it was called Green County Garden Supply.

"I never realized how much of our town was named 'green' until this week!" Izzy said, laughing along with Miguel while she placed her bike in the rack and followed the others inside.

"Good morning, Grace," Mr. Davis greeted one of the workers.

"Hi Mr. Davis," she replied. "How can I help you today?"

"We are looking for supplies to exclude rodents from our homes: specifically, door sweeps, steel wool, and caulking."

"Your timing is perfect," Grace said. "I just moved all that stuff to the front of the store and moved all the rat poison to the back of the store to try and get people to use less of it."

"How about moving all the rat poison right out of the store?" Brooke suggested. Izzy flashed her a look and Brooke quickly apologized to Grace for being rude.

"No need to apologize. You are right, and more people need to speak up about it," Grace said. "You wouldn't believe how much poison we sell. Everyone thinks their one bottle won't matter, but it all adds up."

Grace looked at the kids and noticed Miguel. "I don't remember you in here before. What's your name?"

"I'm Miguel. I'm Izzy's pen pal from Nicaragua. I'm here for a visit."

"Nicaragua? What a beautiful country."

"Thank you. It really is a beautiful country. Unfortunately, we also use too many chemicals.

And we have a problem you don't have."

"What's that?" Brooke asked. "Are the cracks in the houses bigger?"

"Well yes, there is that," Miguel said. "But what I'm thinking of is actually worse than that. Many of the chemicals that are sold have the *instrucciones* for diluting them in English. Since many of the people buying them can't read English, they use them full-strength."

"What's diluting?" Zack asked.

"Diluting," Grace answered, is when you make something weaker by mixing it with water or some other liquid. Many chemicals are supposed to be diluted to just a fraction of the strength they are sold at before using."

"But people use them full-strength because they just don't know," Miguel added.

"That's horrible!" Brooke said. "Don't you feel like giving up?"

"Never," Miguel said. "I will never give up on the animals I love."

"I like your attitude," Grace said. "My partner

gets really down thinking about all the attacks on nature and wildlife but I tell her, never give up."

"Speaking of not giving up, we'd better get to work," Mr. Davis said. He paid for the supplies and they biked to their first stop: the home of Izzy and Zack's Grandma Pearl.

"Bean! Little Z! Otto!" Grandma Pearl greeted Izzy, Zack, and Zack's penguin when they stepped inside her house. "And oh, hello Brooke and Tai. Hello Mr. Davis. And who is this?"

"Grandma, this is Miguel," Izzy said. "My pen pal who is visiting this week."

"He's been here all week and you're just bringing him here now to meet me? What took you so long?" she asked. "Come in. Come in. What can I do for you all?"

"We are here to help you," Izzy said. "We're going to inspect your house for rodent openings and close off any we find so rodents can't get in."

"That sounds fantastic," she said. "This must be a Nature Club project. What can I do to help?"

"You need to relax in your hammock and let us

do the work," Izzy said.

"I love it. But I'll need someone to relax with. How about Miguel? He can tell me stories about Nicaragua."

"That would be *perfecto*," Miguel said. "I would love to see your garden."

So Grandma Pearl sat outside with Miguel, who told her about the birds and volcanoes and festivals in Nicaragua until the rest of the crew emerged from the house.

"All done!" Izzy said.

"Was there much work you needed to do?" Grandma Pearl asked.

"Tons," Zack said.

Mr. Davis laughed. "Given how long you've lived in this house—is it fifty years?"

"Fifty-seven," Grandma Pearl answered.

"Well, given that, it wasn't bad at all," Mr. Davis said.

Grandma Pearl thanked the group for the work and Miguel for the company and they got back on their bikes and headed to the Philipses' house. That house was quicker, and from there they went to Brooke's house, and then finally back to the Davises' house.

At each house, they added door sweeps to close off cracks, stuffed steel wool into openings, and added caulk where needed to seal off little holes. When they were done with the Davises' house, they sat down for a cold drink.

"Well done, team!" Mr. Davis said. "I believe we're finished."

"What about the house cleaning?" Miguel asked Mr. Davis.

He laughed. "The house cleaning will have to be done by each family. I've got my hands full keeping my own house clean."

"I hate cleaning," Brooke said.

"Me too," Zack said.

"If you think of it as a way to keep poisons out of nature, you might hate it a little less," Miguel suggested.

". . . which reminds me," Mr. Davis said. "When cleaning, please be sure to use non-toxic supplies."

"Got it," Brooke said while the others nodded.

The group split up so everyone could get to work at their own home. Izzy and Miguel cleaned the Philipses' house while Mrs. Philips made dinner and Zack took a turn entertaining Carson. After dinner, Mrs. Philips put Carson to bed and then they all cleaned the rest of the house until they were done.

"You kids must be exhausted after the day you've had," Mrs. Philips said.

"Yes, but I would like to call my parents before going to bed. May I please use your phone again?" Miguel asked.

"Of course," Mrs. Philips said and handed him her phone.

Miguel dialed and went outside to talk.

"*Hola*," his mother answered.

"*Es Miguel*," he said.

"*Mijo!*" his mother exclaimed. She wanted to hear about everything Miguel was doing.

"There's so much to tell," Miguel said. He told

her all about making bat and owl boxes, installing exclusion devices, and even cleaning. Miguel said he felt great because that day, they had made a difference—at least locally.

"Wow, what a great day you've had!" Señora Ramirez said. "It sounds like you could use a good night's sleep."

When they hung up, Miguel tiptoed into Zack's room and put on his headlamp to read more about California mammals. But then he thought better of it, laid down, and fell into a deep sleep.

14

When Izzy, Zack, and Miguel convened for breakfast Friday morning, they were met with a surprise.

"A man named Victor called from the local radio station," Mrs. Philips said. "He's going to do a show about rat poison, and he's going to record it this morning over at Ruby's Rehab. He invited you kids from the Nature Club to be there to participate."

"A real radio show?" Zack said. "That's so cool."

"Do the others know?" Izzy asked her mom.

"He said you should tell everyone in the club," Mrs. Philips said.

"Awesome!" Zack said.

The three kids gobbled down their breakfasts, grabbed their bikes, and pedaled over to get Brooke. From there, all four kids rode over to get

Tai, and from there, the whole group biked over to Ruby's.

When they arrived and went around to the back, they saw Ruby, Janet Helling, Victoria Perez, a dark-haired man, and a red-haired woman sitting in folding chairs in a screened-in porch, talking and laughing.

"G'day, kids!" Ruby called, walking out into the yard to greet them.

"Good morning," Miguel said. "Is Clementine better?"

"She's doing a lot better, but she still has a ways to go," Ruby answered. "Why don't you kids go see her and then come join us so I can introduce you?"

The kids ran to see Clementine and breathed a sigh of relief when they saw she looked more energetic than the day before. Even her eyes looked brighter.

They then went to join the others. Victoria and Janet greeted them when they entered the porch and then Ruby introduced them to the two strangers.

"Kids, this is Matthew and Jamie. They are here to record the radio show, 'Coffee Break.'"

"Actually, it will be live," Matthew said.

"Live?" Ruby said. "You mean it will play over the radio as we are being interviewed?"

"That's exactly right," Jamie said with a smile. "But don't worry—you'll do great."

"Oh, now I'm nervous. Well anyway, Matthew and Jamie, this is Izzy, Zack, Brooke, Tai, and Miguel from the Nature Club."

"It is a pleasure to meet you," Matthew said with a smile. "I'm so impressed with your work. Victoria, Janet, and Ruby have all told us great stories about you kids."

"Thanks!" Brooke said while the others smiled.

"And thanks for letting us come," Izzy added.

"I have long been wanting to do a show on the hazards of rat poison, but I never had the right hook," Matthew said. "Grace called me last night and told me about the bobcat and I knew the time was right for the show. I'll interview Ruby about the poison and the rehab work, and then Victoria about the rodents, and then . . . ," he turned to Miguel, "I'd like to interview you about the boxes and exclusion work."

"Me? Live?" Miguel asked.

"Ruby told me how passionate you are about making a difference and how expert you are at conveying the message of the importance of conservation. That's a gift. So I'd like to interview you, too."

"I don't think . . . ," Miguel started, but he was interrupted by a chorus of "You have to!" "You'd be perfect!" and "Please do it!" from his friends.

"You might not have a choice," Jamie said, laughing.

"But I'm not even wearing a suit," Miguel said.

"Good thing this is radio. As in, not television," Brooke joked.

"Good point," Miguel said with a smile.

"Okay now," Jamie said, "this is how it's going to work." She then explained where they would stand, the questions Matthew would ask, and how long it would take. Ruby asked Matthew to call the bobcat number forty-two instead of Clementine, because she didn't believe wild animals should be named.

"Why not?" Matthew asked.

"Because I reckon they shouldn't be treated as pets. They're wild," she said.

"Okay. I promise," Matthew said. Then he tossed out a few practice questions until it was time to start.

Matthew started the show off by introducing Ruby. She explained how rat poison works, and what it does to the animals. She explained how it moves through the food chain and how many non-target wildlife species, pets, and children are accidentally poisoned. She said it happens to a range of animals, including eagles, owls, hawks, bears, snakes, badgers, coyotes, and especially cats. She talked about the irony of removing nature's rodent control to control rodents.

Then Matthew said, "Tell me about Clementine." Ruby raised one eyebrow and

Matthew mouthed, "Oops." The kids covered their mouths to stifle their laughs.

Ruby said, "Number forty-two is a bobcat the county biologist brought in a few days ago." She then continued by talking about number forty-two's symptoms, treatment, and the expected time it would take for the bobcat to fully recover.

"Clementine is the forty-second animal you've treated this year?" Matthew asked, then smacked his right palm against his forehead and mouthed, "I'm sorry."

"She is," Ruby answered, mouthing back to him, "You're a fool."

Matthew looked stunned and quickly turned to Victoria to ask about rodents. "We all care greatly about the secondary victims of poisoning, like hawks, and the accidental victims, like children, but what about the rodents? Should we care about them?"

Victoria smiled. "Absolutely," she said, and then talked about how helpful they are in aerating soil, eating insects, and being food for predators.

Matthew turned to Miguel and asked about how to take action and why it was important. Miguel talked about the boxes, how to install door sweeps, and how good it feels to be a helpful part of the web of life.

Matthew turned back to Ruby, who slipped him a note saying, "Don't say Clementine. Say number forty-two."

Matthew took a deep breath and let it out slowly. He looked at Ruby, smiled, and said, "Ruby, its great these kids are making a difference. They're a role model for all of us."

"I reckon they are," Ruby agreed.

"Now, Ruby," Matthew said. "I would like to ask you about your rehab work. Is it correct that if someone in town finds an injured animal, the best thing to do is bring it here?"

Now it was Ruby's turn to take a deep breath followed by a slow exhale. "Rehab work is important and has its place, but our goal should always be keeping wildlife wild. Rehabilitation can work but has many limitations. It is expensive, time-consuming, takes heaps of space, requires special training and licensing, and only works for some animals with certain injuries. More importantly, it requires taking a wild animal into captivity, and that should only be done as a last resort."

"What's the take-home message there?" Matthew asked.

"It's that we rehabilitators need everyone else to try and make our jobs obsolete by preventing problems from happening in the first place," Ruby answered.

"What's the most common question you get?" Matthew asked. Ruby explained that she got many calls a day from people worried that baby animals had been abandoned—birds, deer, even elephant seals.

"Should they bring them in?" Matthew asked.

"No way," Ruby explained. "In the majority of cases, the babies aren't abandoned. They are either learning to fly or waiting for a parent to bring them food. Picking them up and bringing them to me is creating a problem where one didn't exist."

"Interesting," Matthew said. "Is the use of rat poison the biggest thing you worry about in terms of humans impacting wildlife?"

"Rat poison, insect poison, plant poison—I worry about all of it. Climate change, roads, noise and light disturbance, and habitat loss, too. But the thing I worry about most is the amount of plastic that's going into the ocean because it is so preventable. I've had to treat way too many animals whose guts are full of it."

"I suppose that's because people aren't recycling enough?" Matthew asked.

"I reckon that's part of it. But really, people use recycling as an excuse for overconsumption. Half of the stuff that is put into recycling isn't recycled and even the stuff that is recycled still takes fuels to transport and water to process and on and on. To me, plastic bags are the worst, with plastic bottles being a close second. Heaps of them are finding their way into the oceans."

"So, taking a cue from the Nature Club, what would you ask our listeners to consider doing?" Matthew asked.

"I'd ask them to think of themselves as one part of an interconnected network of life and to take that into consideration with every action they take. There are more than seven billion of us. What each of us does, matters. Every one of our actions has an impact. No one is perfect, but we all need to try," Ruby said, slapping her hand onto her thigh.

Matthew turned to Miguel to get the last word. Miguel, however, was lost in thought. *How many plastic bottles did I use just on this trip?*

"Miguel," Brooke whispered and nudged him. "Matthew's talking to you."

Miguel looked over at Matthew wide-eyed.

"Let me repeat that question for the audience," Matthew said while shaking his head. "I understand your mother is a leader in getting coffee growers to use less chemicals. Can you tell us anything about that?"

Miguel's face lit up. He talked about his mother's work and said that she was even giving a talk that very night on the topic. The best part, he said, was that she hasn't just helped birds—she has also helped howler monkeys.

"Howler monkeys?" Matthew said. "Now there is something to be excited about." Matthew asked if the talk was open to the public. Miguel said it was and gave the time and address. Matthew then made some closing statements and turned off the microphone.

"That's a wrap," Jamie said. "Nice job!"

"How about you all stay for a cold drink?" Ruby asked Matthew and Jamie.

"Oh, we can't," Matthew said. "Always on the move. But thanks." And just like that, they were up and gone.

15

"How about the rest of you stay so we can celebrate with a drink?" Ruby asked the kids after walking Matthew and Jamie to their cars.

"Great. I'm thirsty!" Tai said. "How 'bout you, Miguel? You must be thirsty after all that talking."

"You know what? That interview did make me thirsty," Miguel said. "But I would like to have some tap water in a cup, please. I'm so ashamed at how many bottles I've added to the world's waste instead of drinking tap water this week."

"Give yourself a break," Ruby said. "No one is perfect. And no one wants to be perfect. The main thing is to do your best, and when you learn there is something you've been doing that you could do better, you give it a try. I reckon you kids are terrific."

"I second that," Victoria said.

"If I got mad at myself every time I realized I was making a mistake, I'd be a pretty angry person," Janet added. "We are all works in progress."

"Thanks," Miguel said, blushing.

"Anyway, how about some lemonade?" Ruby asked. "I'll make it with lemons from my tree and cold water from the tap."

"That sounds great!" Brooke said, nudging Miguel.

"That does sound great," Miguel agreed.

After drinking freshly squeezed lemonade, the kids stayed for another hour to help Ruby fix cages and feed some of the animals. Then they biked back to Green County Park.

It was Miguel's last full day, so they swam in the creek, wrote in their journals, and even got in a game of soccer at the nearby field.

At five o'clock, Miguel realized he needed to head back to the Philipses' house so he could call his mom and wish her luck before her talk.

"You can't leave!" Brooke said. "This is our last

full day together."

"This week sure went fast," Tai added.

"It did. I'm really going to miss all of you after I go home," Miguel said.

"How about you all bike over to the train station tomorrow to wish him a safe trip?" Izzy suggested. "Then we don't have to be sad saying good-bye right now."

"I can," Tai said. "How 'bout it, Brooke?"

"I'm in!"

Everyone headed home and Miguel asked Mrs. Philips if he could borrow her phone one last time before dinner.

"Of course," she said, handing it to him.

Since Señora Ramirez's voice was tense when she answered the phone, Miguel could tell she was nervous.

"*Mamá*, are you okay?" he asked.

"*Ay Mijo*, I am just nervous."

"*Mamá*, you are the best speaker ever. You will do great."

"I hope," she said.

Miguel could hear his father saying it was time to go to the banquet.

"I wish I had more time to hear about your day," his mother said. "Do you promise to tell me all about it tomorrow?"

"Of course. We have the whole trip back to Nicaragua to talk," he said. "Tell *Papá* I say hi. And *Mamá*, good luck! *Te amo*."

"*Te amo, Mijo*."

Miguel went back into the house and enjoyed his last meal with the Philipses. The kids told Mrs. Philips all about the radio interview and what they'd learned about bottles. She said she was proud of them and wondered what she could do to make a positive change.

Miguel played with his fork for a minute and took a deep breath. "Actually," he said. "I do have an idea."

Everyone turned to Miguel and waited for him to say more.

"There is a bright light that shines at night. I think it would be better if it was either off or shielded to only shine downward," he said.

"Ohhh. Right," Izzy said, nodding her head. "I hadn't even though about that until now."

"Has it been disturbing your sleep?" Mrs. Philips asked.

"No, but I'm worried about the nocturnal animals and migrating birds. It might be disturbing them."

"Oh my gosh, you're right. Just like Ruby said on the radio today," Mrs. Philips said. "This isn't our home—we're just renting it for the summer—but I bet the owners have it on an automatic timer to go on at night for safety."

"Safety from what?" Miguel asked.

"Burglars," Mrs. Philips answered.

"But the light is shining up. Ruby taught us lights that shine up not only disturb wildlife, but actually make it easier for burglars to sneak around because of all the shadows they make. Apparently, it's even easier to sneak about in shadows than in darkness."

"Hmm. That's a good point," Mrs. Philips said.

I'll unplug the timer tonight and buy a cover for the light tomorrow. I've seen some nice ones at a shop downtown that direct all the light downward. That would be much more effective. It would also be a nice gift to the owners for renting us their house."

"That would be great," Miguel said.

"I agree. Now we can all go to sleep knowing we're working to make things better for wildlife," Mrs. Philips said. "Now all of you get a good night's sleep. Miguel has a big day of traveling tomorrow."

16

Clementine stood up to stretch. There had been a lot of noise and human visitors that day, but now it was once again quiet. She moved slowly, pacing back and forth within the confines of her large pen at the rehab center.

After a few laps, she sat down near a dish and lapped up some warm water. Then she stood, stretched, and sat back down. It was time to groom. She licked her way carefully down one leg, cleaning her fur with her raspy tongue. Then she rested. She would groom the other leg when her energy returned.

17

On Saturday, Mrs. Philips made waffles as she sipped her organic, shade-grown coffee. "Where did the week go? I can't believe I haven't made these for you yet," she said.

They smelled delicious. "Can I help?" Miguel asked. He was, as usual, the first kid up.

"How about if you set the table?" Mrs. Philips said as she handed him silverware and cloth napkins.

As the scent filled the house, Izzy and Zack appeared. "Waffles!" Zack said. "Can I have extra whipped cream on mine?"

"Why not?" Mrs. Philips said as she handed out plates with waffles to each kid.

"I can't believe this is breakfast and not dessert," Miguel said. Then he took a bite. "Wow.

Delicious. This has been the best week ever. Thank you so much."

"Miguel, we've loved having you. I hope one day Izzy can spend a week at your house in Nicaragua."

"And me," Zack said.

"And you," Mrs. Philips said with a smile.

Miguel ate three giant waffles piled high with whipped cream before his stomach gurgled. "Oops. I think I've had enough."

"Sounds like we're sending you back the way you came," Izzy said. They all laughed.

"We'd better get going down to the train station," Mrs. Philips said.

They loaded up into the car and headed down just as the train was pulling into the station. Miguel could see his parents waving through one of the train windows.

His mother got off first, followed by his father, who was carrying their suitcases.

"*Mijo!*" Señora Ramirez exclaimed and pulled Miguel in a big hug.

"*Mamá!* I missed you so much," he said.

"And I missed you!"

Then Miguel's father walked up.

"Ah! Miguel," his father said, followed by, "How are you?" in stilted English.

"*Papá!*" Miguel said to his father and gave him a big hug.

Then Señora Ramirez turned to Mrs. Philips and gave her a hug, "Thank you for taking care of Miguel. He had such a great week."

"Oh, he was terrific. We so enjoyed having him," Mrs. Philips said. "How was your conference? Miguel said you gave the closing talk last night!"

"I did and you won't believe this . . . ," Señora Ramirez said, her eyes twinkling.

"What happened, *Mamá*?" Miguel asked.

"The governor of California came to my talk! And he stayed afterward to ask questions. He said he had no idea that the way crops are grown can have such an impact on the environment and the workers. And . . . there's more. He's going to promote more sustainable practices of growing crops across all of California and a reduced reliance on chemicals!"

Señor Ramirez stood next to her, beaming.

"*Mamá!* I can't believe it. You're amazing."

"No, Miguel. You're amazing. You won't believe what brought him to the conference."

"He wasn't there to hear about organic coffee?"

"Actually, he was, but he didn't know about my talk until that afternoon. He said he was working in Sacramento when his son called. His son had heard a story on the radio about rat poison and how it impacted predators through the food chain. He said you were interviewed about how important it is to reduce our use of poisons throughout the environment and that you mentioned my conference and my talk."

"The governor said that when you talked about the howler monkeys, his son was touched. That's why he called his father, the governor, to tell him about it. The governor canceled his afternoon meetings and drove to San Francisco to hear my talk. He sat in the front row and heard the whole thing. He even laughed at my jokes."

The kids were so excited they were jumping up and down.

"Oh, I almost forgot. He also said the other speaker talked about how much plastic waste is hurting wildlife and gave me a set of refillable water bottles to give all of you." She handed each kid a refillable water bottle with the seal of the state of California on it.

"That's exactly what I need!" Miguel said. "It seems I learned how to make a big difference, but somehow forgot to look at my own little impacts. Thank you!"

"Yes, thanks Señora Ramirez," the others said in unison.

"Now," Mrs. Philips said, "how long do you have before your train leaves to take you back to the airport?"

"At this point, only about twenty minutes."

"Just long enough for a toast!" Brooke said.

They all went to the café, but instead of buying

drinks, the kids all washed their bottles and filled them with tap water. Then they stepped outside just as there was an announcement that the train back to San Francisco would arrive in five minutes.

"We better hurry," Izzy said. All the members of the Nature Club were present and wearing their official T-shirts. They stood in a circle and lifted their water bottles in the air.

"To friendship!" Brooke said.

"And bobcats and all the other predators," Zack said.

"And don't forget their prey and their habitat," Tai said with a grin.

"And to all being part of one beautiful interconnected planet," Izzy added.

"And to making a difference!" Miguel said.

They had a huge group hug. Tai gave Miguel his lucky penny, Miguel gave Zack his soccer ball, and everyone promised to stay in touch. Then the Ramirez family boarded the train and everyone waved until the train was out of sight.

Epilogue

One month later, Clementine tentatively stepped out of a small transport cage at the edge of Green County Park. The ride in the truck from the rehab center to the park had been short, but she didn't know where she was going or what was ahead. When the truck stopped, a woman with a long braid that fell down her back took the cage out of the truck and set it on the ground. She then took off the blankets that had covered the cage and kept the bobcat calm on the drive.

Once the bobcat had her two front paws in the grass, it all felt familiar. She ran off and hid in the bushes until the truck drove away.

Then she emerged. Free. She jumped up high and made dramatic aerial turns as she ran back and forth. She stopped and rolled over and played with the grass using her front paws.

Then she stopped and lifted her head. Her ears turned out to the field. She sat up higher and looked around until she saw it—a gopher.

She approached slowly. The gopher poked its head out of the ground and then dove back in. The bobcat looked inside and then backed off. She found a place to sit and wait. Her tail twitched. The gopher poked its head out again and then, the bobcat pounced.

She missed.

She waited.

The gopher poked its head out again. The bobcat pounced again and jammed her arm down into the hole. This time, she didn't miss. Wild and free, the bobcat sat back to enjoy her reward.

Notes on Bobcats

by Miguel Ramirez

Bobcats, also known as Lynx rufus, usually have tan to grayish-brown coats with black spots. Their pointed ears have black tips and black tufts of hair. They have white chins and underbellies, yellow eyes, and black-tipped, stubby (or "bobbed") tails. Adults weigh an average of about nine kilograms (or twenty pounds).

Bobcats are found in Canada, throughout the United States, and into central Mexico. Unfortunately for me, they are not in Central America even though they are adaptable and live in a range of environments.

Bobcats have great hearing and vision, are excellent climbers, and can even swim! They normally spend their time alone and are crepuscular, which means they are active at twilight, but they'll switch to be day-active to catch their prey, if needed.

Bobcats are carnivores; their favorite foods are rabbits and hares. They also hunt birds, deer, bats, and rodents, which is why they can get poisoned by rodenticides.

***

To keep bobcats and other animals safe

from being poisoned, here are some ways you can keep rodents away without using rodenticides:

- Plug all openings in buildings greater than six millimeters (or ¼ inch) to keep rodents from entering.

- Use wire netting and metal cages to protect plants from gophers.

- Avoid planting hedgerows near potential entryways for rodents, to discourage them from using the area.

- Install owl boxes to encourage these natural rodent predators to use the area.

- Keep outdoor areas clear of food and garbage, and even crumbs so they don't attract rodents.

Questions to Consider:

1. Miguel lives in Nicaragua. Can you find his country on a map or globe?

2. Miguel lives in a different time zone than California. Have you ever been in a different time zone than the one where you live?

3. Miguel wanted to make a big difference in the world. Do you think he did in the end?

4. Can you think of a way you can make a positive difference in the world?

5. Have you ever had an impact on someone or something else unintentionally?

6. Has anyone ever had an unintentional impact on you?

Join the Nature Club
for more adventures!

www.natureclubbooks.com

Acknowledgments

I am grateful to Wren Sturdevant, Max Sturdevant, John Sturdevant, Elettra Cudignotto, Rachelle Dyer, Allan Mazur, Polly Mazur, Julie Mazur Tribe, Matthew Tribe, Salvadora Morales, Lisa Rhudy, Michael Ross, Molly Stephens, Chuck Carter, Jenny Mahon, Ceci Jackson, Leslie Paladino, Emma Irving, Jessica Santina, and Sarah Hoggatt for their help and encouragement.

I am also grateful to Miguel Ordeñana, community science manager at the Natural History Museum of Los Angeles County, who generously provided expert review.

About the Author

Rachel Mazur, Ph.D., is the author of *Speaking of Bears* (Globe Pequot, 2015), the award-winning picture book *If You Were a Bear* (Sequoia Natural History Association, 2008), and many articles for scientific and trade publications. She is passionate about writing stories to connect kids with nature—and inspiring them to protect it. Rachel lives with her husband and two children in El Portal, California, where she oversees the wildlife program at Yosemite National Park.

To learn more about The Nature Club series, please visit natureclubbooks.com.

To learn more about the art of Elettra Cudignotto, please visit elettracudignotto.com.

To learn more about the art of Rachelle Dyer, please visit rachellepaintings.com.

Made in the USA
Middletown, DE
26 September 2020